Earwig and the Witch

Books by Diana Wynne Jones

Chrestomanci Series
Charmed Life
The Magicians of Caprona
Witch Week
The Lives of
Christopher Chant
Mixed Magics
Conrad's Fate
The Pinhoe Egg

Howl Series
Howl's Moving Castle
Castle in the Air
House of Many Ways

The Dalemark Quartet
Cart and Cwidder
Drowned Ammet
The Spellcoats
The Crown of Dalemark

Archer's Goon
Black Maria
Dogsbody
Eight Days of Luke

Enchanted Glass
The Homeward Bounders
The Merlin Conspiracy
Deep Secret
The Dark Lord of Derkholm
Year of the Griffin
The Ogre Downstairs
Power of Three
A Tale of Time City
Wilkins' Tooth
The Game
The Islands of Chaldea
(with Ursula Jones)

For older readers
Fire and Hemlock
Hexwood
The Time of the Ghost

For younger readers
Wild Robert
Earwig and the Witch
Vile Visitors
Freaky Families

DIANA WYNNE JONES

Earwig and the Witch

Illustrated by Marion Lindsay

HarperCollins *Children's Books*

First published in 2011 by HarperCollins *Children's Books*
This film tie-in edition published in 2021 by
HarperCollins *Children's Books*
HarperCollins *Children's Books* is a division
of HarperCollinsPublishers Ltd,
1 London Bridge Street
London SE1 9GF

www.harpercollins.co.uk

1

HarperCollins*Publishers*
1st Floor, Watermarque Building, Ringsend Road
Dublin 4, Ireland

Text copyright © Diana Wynne Jones 2011
Inside illustrations copyright © Marion Lindsay 2011
Cover art © 2020 NHK, NEP, Studio Ghibli
Cover design based on film poster © lesaliens.com

ISBN: 978-0-00-847523-9

Diana Wynne Jones and Marion Lindsay assert the moral
rights to be identified as the author and illustrator
of the work respectively.

A CIP catalogue record for this title is
available from the British Library

Printed and bound in England by
CPI Group (UK) Ltd, Croydon CR0 4YY

MIX
Paper from
responsible sources
FSC™ C007454

FSC
www.fsc.org

To Leo and Max

Bella Yaga

Mandrake

Earwig

Custard

Thomas

Chapter One

At St Morwald's Home for Children it was the day when people who wanted to be foster parents came to see which children they might want to take home with them.

Chapter One

"How *boring*!" Earwig said to her friend Custard. The two of them were lined up in the dining room with the bigger children. Earwig thought this whole afternoon was an utter waste of time. She was perfectly happy at St Morwald's. She liked the clean smell of polish everywhere and the bright sunny rooms. She liked the people there. This was because everyone, from Mrs Briggs the Matron to the newest and smallest children, did exactly what Earwig wanted. If Earwig fancied shepherd's pie for lunch, she could get the cook to make

it for her. If she wanted a new red
sweater, Mrs Briggs hurried out and
bought it for her. If she wanted to play
Hide-and-Seek in the dark, all the
children played even though some of
them were frightened. Earwig was never
frightened. She had a very strong
personality.

There were noises from the playroom
next door where the babies and toddlers
were lined up too. Earwig could hear
people crying out, "Oh, isn't she sweet!"
and "Oh, just look at this little one's
eyes!"

"Disgusting!" Earwig muttered.

"What cheek!" Earwig liked most of the babies and all the toddlers, but she did not think they were made to be admired. They were people, not dolls.

"It's all right for you," her friend
Custard said. "Nobody ever chooses
you."

Earwig liked Custard best out of
everyone at St Morwald's. He always did

exactly what she said. His only fault was that he got scared rather too often. She said soothingly, "You never get chosen either. Don't worry."

"But people hover over me," Custard said. "Sometimes they *almost* choose me." Then he added, very daringly, "Don't you ever want to be chosen and go to live somewhere else, Earwig?"

"No," Earwig said firmly. But she wondered about it. Might it just be fun to go and live in an ordinary house the way other children did? Then she thought of all the numbers of people in

St Morwald's who all did exactly what she wanted, and she realised that in an ordinary house there would only be two or three people, or six at the most. That was far too few to be interesting. "No," she said. "Anyone who chose me would have to be very unusual."

Just then, Mrs Briggs came hurrying through from the playroom, looking flustered. "The bigger ones are in here," she said. "If you'd like to follow me, I'll tell you the names and a little bit about each child."

Earwig had only time to whisper

Chapter One

warningly to Custard, "Remember to cross your eyes like I taught you!" before a very strange couple followed Mrs Briggs into the dining room. Earwig could see they had tried to make themselves look ordinary, but she knew they were not. Not in the least. The woman had one brown eye and one

blue one, and a raggety, ribby look to her
face. It was not a nice face. The woman
had tried to make it nicer by doing her
hair in blue-rinsed curls and putting on
a lot of purple lipstick. This did not go
with her brown tweed suit or her bright
green sweater. And none of it went with
her big red hat or her sky-blue
high-heeled boots.

As for the man – the first time
Earwig looked at him, he looked like
anyone you might pass in the street. The
second time she looked, she could hardly
see him at all. He was like a long, black

17

streak in the air. After that, every time she looked at the man, he seemed taller, and taller still, and his face seemed grimmer and more frowning. And he seemed to have long ears. By the time the man and the woman were standing in front of Custard, Earwig was almost sure that the man was nine feet tall and that he *did* have two somethings sticking up from his head. The somethings could have been ears, but Earwig rather thought they were horns.

"This little boy is John Coster," Mrs Briggs was saying. Earwig was glad she was not Custard. "His parents were both killed in a fire," Mrs Briggs explained. "So sad!"

Custard usually scowled when Mrs Briggs said this kind of thing. He hated people saying his life was sad. But Earwig could see he was so frightened of the strange couple that he could not even frown. And he had quite forgotten to cross his eyes.

Before Earwig could nudge Custard to remind him to cross his eyes, the strange couple lost interest in him. They moved on to stand in front of Earwig. Custard went white with relief.

Mrs Briggs sighed. "And this is Erica Wigg," she said hopelessly. Mrs Briggs

never could quite pin down just why it
was that nobody ever wanted to take
Earwig home with them. Earwig was
skinny. Her front teeth and her elbows
stuck out rather, and she insisted on
doing her hair in two bunches that stuck
out too, just like her elbows and her
teeth. But Mrs Briggs had known far
worse-looking children who seemed to
be wanted by everyone. What Mrs Briggs
did not know was that Earwig was very
good at making herself look unlovable.
It was something that she did quite
quietly, on the inside of her face, and she

always did it, because she was quite happy to stay at St Morwald's.

She made herself look unlovable now. She thought these two people were the most awful she had ever seen. They stared at her grimly.

"Erica has been with us since she was a baby," Mrs Briggs said brightly, seeing the way they were looking. She did not say, because she always thought it was so peculiar,

that Earwig had been left on the
doorstep of St Morwald's early one
morning with a note pinned to her
shawl. The note said:

GOT THE OTHER TWELVE WITCHES
ALL CHASING ME. I'LL BE BACK
FOR HER WHEN I'VE SHOOK THEM
OFF. IT MAY TAKE YEARS. HER
NAME IS EARWIG.

Mrs Briggs and the Assistant Matron
had scratched their heads over this. The
Assistant Matron said, "If this mother's
one of thirteen, she must be a witch who
has annoyed the rest of her coven."

"Nonsense!" said Mrs Briggs.

"But," said the Assistant Matron, "this means that the baby could be a witch as well."

Mrs Briggs said, "Nonsense!" again. "There are no such things as witches."

Mrs Briggs had never told Earwig about the note, nor that her name really *was* Earwig. She thought it was probably a bad joke. Earwig was not a real name. So Mrs Briggs had written "Erica Wigg" firmly on Earwig's birth certificate and kept her mouth shut about the rest.

Meanwhile Earwig was making

herself look as unlovable as she could.
Custard was edging away from her and
even Mrs Briggs was thinking what a
pity it was that Earwig's charming
nature never seemed to show when it
mattered. And the strange couple were
looking as if they thought Earwig was
quite hateful.

The woman turned to the nine-foot
man and looked up at him from under
her red hat. "Well?" she said. "What
does the Mandrake think?"

"I think probably," he answered in a
deep, angry voice.

The woman turned to Mrs Briggs.
"We'll take this one," she said, just as if
Earwig was a melon or a joint of meat on
the market.

Mrs Briggs was so surprised that she
rocked back on her feet. Before she could
recover, Earwig said, "No she won't. I
want to stay here."

"Don't be silly, dear," said Mrs Briggs.
"You know how much everyone here
wants to see you living with a real
family, just like other children."

"I don't want to," said Earwig. "I want
to stay with Custard."

"Now, dear," said Mrs Briggs. "These kind people live quite near, in Lime Avenue. I'm sure they'll let you come back to see your friends whenever you want to, and when school starts again you'll be able to see Custard every day."

After that, there seemed nothing Earwig could do but go and help one of the trainee girls pack her things in a bag, while Mrs Briggs took the strange couple to her office to sign forms. Then she had to say goodbye to Custard and hurry after the woman in the red hat and the nine-foot man. The things on his head *were* horns, Earwig was sure. She was surprised nobody else noticed. But mostly she was angry and amazed that, for the first time in her life, somebody was making her do something she didn't want to do. She could not understand it.

"I suppose I'd better think of it as a challenge," she said to herself as they turned into Lime Avenue.

Chapter Two

Earwig was not at all surprised to find that the house in Lime Avenue was Number Thirteen. It fitted these people, even if it was only a perfectly ordinary bungalow. The nine-foot man opened the gate and went through a neat garden with diamond-shaped rose-beds in the exact centre of each lawn. The windows of the bungalow were all nice and low, Earwig noticed. They would be easy to climb out of if the challenge got too much for her and she decided to run away.

The man went through the front door first and walked away down the hall, saying, "I got you what you wanted. Now I don't want to be disturbed any more."

Earwig did not see where he went then, because the woman opened the

nearest door on the right and slung
Earwig's bag inside it. "You'll be
sleeping in there," she said. Earwig had
just a glimpse of a small bare bedroom,
before the woman shut the door and
took her big red hat off. As she hung it
carefully on a peg, she said, "Now let's
get a few things straight. My name is
Bella Yaga and I am a witch. I've
brought you here because I need another
pair of hands. If you work hard and do
what you're told like a good girl, I shan't
do anything to hurt you. If—"

Earwig saw that this was going to be

a very big challenge indeed, far bigger
than any she had faced at St Morwald's.
That was all right. She liked a challenge.
And somewhere at the back of her mind,
Earwig had always hoped that perhaps
one day she might find a person who
could teach her some magic. "That's all
right," she interrupted. If you want to
make somebody do what you want, it is
very important to start with them in the
right way. Earwig knew all about that.
"It's all right," she said. "I didn't think
you looked like a Foster Mother. So it's
settled then. You agree to teach me

magic and I agree to stay here and be your assistant."

She could tell Bella Yaga had expected to have to bully and threaten her. "Well, that's settled then," she said crossly. She looked quite put out. "You'd better come in here and start work." She led Earwig through the door on the left.

Earwig looked round and tried not to sniff too loudly. She had never seen a place so dirty. Since she was used to the airy rooms and clean polished floors of St Morwald's, it was quite a shock. Everything was covered with dust. There

was a kind of sludge on the floor made
of old dirt, green mould and the remains
of spells – which mostly seemed to be
little white bones and small, black,
rotting things. The sludge rose to a hill
in one corner, on which perched a rusty
black cauldron with green flames

flickering under it. The smell of burning
was awful. More smelly things, like
dusty bottles and old brown packets,
some of them spilling, lay about on the
long dirty table, or were chucked
higgledy-piggledy on the shelves. All the
bowls and jugs stacked on the floor were

covered with grime or brown slime.

Earwig closed her nose against the smell, wondering if witchcraft really *needed* so many rotting things. She thought that, when she had learnt enough, she would be a new kind of witch. A clean one. Meanwhile, she looked round the room and was puzzled to see that it seemed to be at least the size of the whole bungalow.

Bella Yaga chuckled at the look on Earwig's face. "Come along, girl," she said. "You're not here to stare. If you don't like it, you can clean it later. For now, I want you at this table, powdering those rats' bones for me." When Earwig came over to the table, getting her ankles tangled with two dead snakes on the way, Bella Yaga said, "Now there's one great rule in this house. You must learn it straight away. You must on no account *ever* disturb the Mandrake."

"You mean the man with the horns?" Earwig said.

"He hasn't got horns!" Bella Yaga said angrily. "At least, most of the time, he hasn't. He gets those when he's disturbed."

"What else happens when he's disturbed?" Earwig asked.

She thought Bella Yaga shuddered at the idea. "Awful things," the witch said. "If you're lucky, you won't find out. Now get to work."

Soon Earwig was pounding away with a heavy pestle in a little stone bowl. At first the small white bones in the bowl went *crunch*, *crunch*. After an hour, they were white powder and went *spluff*, *spluff*, but Bella Yaga said the powder had to be finer than the finest flour and she made Earwig go on pounding. By

this time, Earwig's arms ached and she
was bored. Bella Yaga would not tell her
why she was having to make the powder.
She would not answer any of Earwig's
questions at all.

Earwig saw quite clearly that Bella
Yaga was not going to teach her magic.

Chapter Two

She just wanted Earwig to do the hard work. Earwig knew she would have to do something about that, as soon as she knew enough about Bella Yaga and her bungalow and all her ways. So she went on pounding at the powder and kept her eyes and ears open.

The only other living creature in the workroom was a black cat, who spent his time lurking miserably in the warmth behind the rusty cauldron. Every so often Bella Yaga would run her finger down a page of the greasy little book on the table beside her and

42

mutter, "Calls for a familiar here." Then she would march over to the cauldron shouting, "Come on, Thomas! Time to do your stuff!"

Thomas always tried to escape. Once Bella Yaga caught him with only a short scuffle, but most times he fled round the walls of the room with Bella Yaga pounding after him, bawling, "Do what you're told, Thomas, or I shall give you worms!" When she caught Thomas, she marched back to the table carrying him by the scruff of his neck and dumped him beside the greasy book. Thomas

crouched there in an angry, ruffled heap
until Bella Yaga had finished that part
of her spell. Then he fled back behind
the cauldron again.

Earwig could see that the greasy
book had all Bella Yaga's spells in it.
From where Earwig stood, it reminded
her of the book of recipes the cook at St
Morwald's kept, except that this book
was a lot dirtier. The third time Bella
Yaga went pounding round the room
after Thomas, Earwig kept hammering
away at the powder with one hand and
pulled the little book nearer with the

other hand. Still banging away
one-handed, she turned the pages.

A Spell to Win First Prize in a Dog Show
was the one Bella Yaga was working on
at the moment. The next page was *To
Make Next-Door's Dahlias Die* and the
page after that was *Love Potion for the
Boy Next Door*. That was where Bella
Yaga came striding back to the table
carrying the curled-up, dangling
Thomas. Earwig hurriedly pushed the
book back to the other side of the table
and went back to thumping at the
powder with both hands.

By supper time, Earwig had seen about a quarter of the spells in the book, but not one of them seemed of any use to *her*. She thought for quite a while about a spell called *To Make a Skateboard Do Tricks*, but although that spell sounded fun, there seemed nothing in it that would stop Bella Yaga doing something awful to her if she tried it. And that was what she really needed, she thought, as she followed Bella Yaga down the hall to the kitchen. She needed to be safe from Bella Yaga before she could make her do anything.

To Earwig's surprise, the kitchen was

an ordinary kitchen, quite warm and cosy, with the table laid for three and supper steaming on it. There was a large fish on a plate under the table, which Thomas hurried to eat. Earwig looked at the Mandrake. He was looming in a chair at the end of the table, reading a large leather book. He looked like an ordinary man in a bad temper. Even so, he did not look like a man who would have got supper ready.

"And what have the demons brought us today?" Bella Yaga asked in the bright, wheedling voice she always

seemed to use to the Mandrake.

"Pie and chips from Stoke-on-Trent Station Buffet," the Mandrake growled without looking up.

"I hate Station pie," said Bella Yaga.

The Mandrake looked up. His eyes were like dark pits. A spark of red fire glowed, deep down in each pit. "It's my favourite food," he said. The sparks in his eyes flickered and grew.

Earwig quite understood then why she was not to disturb the Mandrake. She was glad that he did not seem to notice she was there.

Chapter Three

For the next day or so, Earwig went about quietly finding out all she could about Thirteen Lime Avenue. It was a very strange place. For a start, there seemed no way to get out at the front.

There was no front door on the inside.
The place where it should have been was
just bare wall. Earwig could see the neat
front garden out of the window in her
little bare bedroom, but when she tried
to open the window, she found there was
no way to open it. It was just glass built
into the wall.

Earwig decided to see that as one more challenge and find another way out. She could get into the back garden easily enough. It was through a door in the kitchen and it was a riot of weeds. Bella Yaga was always sending Earwig out there to pick nettles or bryony berries or deadly nightshade. Every time, Earwig pushed her way through head-high nettles and thistles to a new place in the tangle of giant brambles round the edge, but all that happened was that she got scratched and stung.

"You won't get out that way!" Bella

Yaga said, laughing meanly.

"Why not?" said Earwig.

"Because the Mandrake's got his demons guarding it, of course," Bella Yaga said.

Earwig nodded. That made another challenge. She began to see that she would have to make the Mandrake do what she wanted too, and that would not be easy to do without disturbing him.

She went on exploring. The bungalow was much bigger inside than it had looked from the outside and there was a lot of it to explore. The door next to

Earwig's room led to the bathroom. It was ordinary like the kitchen. Earwig soon found that she was the only person who bothered to wash in it, or clean her teeth. As soon as she was sure, she took the bathroom over and pinned her snapshots of Custard and Mrs Briggs to the cupboard door.

The door beyond the bathroom went into a huge room full of the kind of leather books the Mandrake read at supper. The door at the end of the hall, beside the kitchen door, opened into a dark place with a concrete floor that smelled... well, as if something had died in there. Earwig took a deep breath, held her nose, and tiptoed to the door at the other end. The place beyond there looked like a church, but there was a car – a little Citroën – parked in the middle between the pillars. There was no door to anywhere else from there. Earwig

supposed it must be the garage. She
backed out, rather annoyed.

Apart from these rooms and Bella
Yaga's workroom, the kitchen was the
only other room Earwig could find.
When she went in there on her first
morning, she was surprised again at how
ordinary it was. Thomas was sitting in
the sun on the windowsill, with his front
paws tucked under him, just like a
normal cat. Bella Yaga was frying bacon
and eggs at the stove.

"Watch carefully," Bella Yaga said to
Earwig. "I shall expect you to cook

Chapter Three

breakfast in the future."

"Yes," said Earwig. "Where do you
sleep? I can't find a door to your
bedroom."

"Mind your own business," said Bella
Yaga.

"What will you do to me if I don't?"
Earwig asked.

She could tell that Bella Yaga had not
expected that question. She looked rather
taken aback and answered with the
same threat she used on Thomas. "I
shall give you worms." Then she seemed
to feel she had better scare Earwig

properly. She added, "Great big blue and purple wriggly worms. So take care, my girl!"

Earwig did not take care. She was quiet and dutiful in the workroom all day. Bella Yaga set her to chopping nettles, mashing poison berries and slicing snakeskins into thin, thin strips. In the afternoons there were always things to count, grains of salt or newts' eyes. Earwig was annoyed again. In the first two days she only managed to look at the book of spells four times, and the only spell that seemed remotely useful

was one headed *To Sharpen the Eyes at Night*. While Earwig wondered how she might use that one, she kept a careful eye on what Bella Yaga did with the things Earwig had chopped and sliced for her. It looked interesting – and easy. Some of the things were boiled in the cauldron and then whipped into lotions with an old, rattly electric mixer. Others were carefully wrapped in small bundles inside a deadly nightshade leaf, which Bella Yaga then tied in special knots with the strips of snakeskin. Earwig would have liked to try doing that too.

"The only thing wrong with magic is that it smells so awful," Earwig said to herself when she was in her own room at night. She sighed. Even the idea of doing a real spell herself did not quite make up for not living at St Morwald's. She missed Custard quite dreadfully. And she was not used to sleeping alone at night. At St Morwald's there had been dormitories with rows of beds. But the thing she missed most was not being able to go to the cook and ask for what she wanted for supper. "I used to be just like the Mandrake, I suppose," Earwig sighed.

"Only he has demons to get him what he wants, lucky thing!"

The only thing that stopped her being really miserable was the cat, Thomas. Somehow he pushed her door open – though Earwig knew she had shut it tightly – and jumped on her bed, where he sat on her feet and purred. Earwig stroked him. His fur was soft and plushy and quite clean, in spite of having been behind the cauldron all day. His purring, rumbling through her toes, was so comforting that Earwig talked to him a lot. Several times she made a mistake and called him Custard. That cheered her up so much that she got out her drawing things and made a very unkind drawing of Bella Yaga. She put in Bella Yaga's odd eyes and blue hair and purple lipstick, and she made her ribby face as ugly as possible. After that, she felt much better. In the morning, she pinned the picture up on the bathroom cupboard and felt better still.

Thomas came and sat on Earwig the next night too. Earwig stroked him.

Then she started to make a drawing of
the Mandrake, as huge and frowning
and horrible as she could make it. She
put dots of red inside his eyes and added
the horns – only they looked more like a
donkey's ears. She would have liked to
put in a demon or two, but she did not

know what demons looked like, so she
went back to making the Mandrake's
face look horrible. But she kept being
distracted in her drawing by a strange
light on the wall of her room. It almost
looked as if the wall was blushing, or
there was a fire deep inside it.

"Whatever *is* that?" she said angrily,
after she had made a mistake on the
Mandrake's mouth the third time.

"It's the Mandrake," said Thomas.
"His den's on the other side of this wall."

Earwig dropped her felt-tip pen and
stared at the cat. His round, light-green

eyes looked calmly back. "You – er – you speak!" she said.

"Of course," said Thomas. "Though not often. I think you should stop that drawing. It's beginning to disturb the Mandrake."

Earwig pushed her paper and pens hurriedly under the covers. "Do you know about spells?" she asked.

"A fair amount. More than you do," said Thomas. "I've seen you looking in her book. The one you really want is near the end. Want me to show you?"

"Yes *please*!" said Earwig.

Chapter Four

"**B**ut just a moment," Earwig added. "How *can* the Mandrake's room be on the other side of this wall? That's the bathroom."

Thomas was in the middle of standing

up and stretching his legs, in pairs. He looked at her over his sleek, black shoulder. "Yes, I know," he said. "But it is, all the same." He finished stretching and sharpened his claws on the bedspread. "Coming?" he said and sprang to the floor.

Earwig pattered after him, out of her room and across the hall. The workroom door was locked. But Thomas stretched up and did some more claw-sharpening near the doorknob. The door quietly opened. Earwig fumbled the lights on and they crept inside.

"Oh, yucky!" Earwig cried out at the feel of the slime under her bare feet.

"Hush. You can lick them clean later." Thomas jumped onto the table and pawed the greasy little book. "Open it at the end and keep turning back until I tell you to stop," he said.

Earwig did so. She turned from *To Make a Plague of Worms*, quickly, because Thomas began shuddering, to *A Thunderstorm to Spoil a Church Fete*, and then to *A Spell to Make a Bus Come on Time*, and *To Preserve the Body from all Magic*, and—

"Hold it there," said Thomas. "That's ours. If we use that, she can't do a thing to either of us."

Earwig looked. The spell took up two pages in small writing. "But Custard – I mean, Thomas – it's got *hundreds* of things in it!"

"All of them are in this room somewhere and we've got all night," Thomas said. "Get going." He sat in front of the book, tail curled round the front of his legs and twitching gently. "You'll need powdered rats' bones, newts' eyes and well-sliced toad for the first stage. While you're doing those, you can start the henbane heating – you have to heat three hairs of a cat's tail in with it and mind you take them *gently*."

For quite half the night, Earwig slithered to and fro in the slime, working far harder than she had ever worked for

Bella Yaga during the day. Thomas sat bent over the book as if he were watching a mouse-hole, calling out the next things the spell needed.

"Belladonna now – that's the fourth bottle along, the one that's not as dusty as the others. Three drops in with the henbane." About halfway through, he said, "Familiar needed. That's all right. I'm here."

"What does that mean?" Earwig gasped. By this time she was pounding gunk with one hand and stirring a gooey green mixture with the other, as if her life depended on it. And perhaps it did, she thought. Bella Yaga was not going to forgive her for this if she found out.

"A familiar is a cat or other animal who is a witch's helper," Thomas said. "The animal needs to be close to the spell to make it work. And," he added

smugly, "a black cat does that best of all."

"Then why do you always run away?" Earwig gasped, mixing and pounding. It was

like trying to pat your head and rub
your stomach at the same time.

"Because I don't like the kind of
spells she does," said Thomas. "They
make me feel as if someone is stroking
me the wrong way. One drip of rose
elixir into the green mix now."

Right near the end there was a nasty
moment when Thomas read out, "Mix
all together in a large bowl and say
words."

"What words?" asked Earwig,
bending over Thomas to look. There
were no words written down in the book.

After '*say words*', the spell went on, '*Spread resulting ointment over every part of your body*.' "WHAT WORDS?" Earwig screamed. "It doesn't *say*!"

"Calm down!" said Thomas, who was looking a little twitchy himself. "They'll be words of binding. I've heard her use about six different words. I think I can remember—"

"You'd better remember, Custard – I mean, Thomas!" Earwig said. "After all this work I've done! Say them all. Every single one you've ever heard!"

"All right," Thomas said, flicking his

tail irritably. "But only if you stop calling me Custard. And you'll have to say them after me exactly as I say them. You're the witch here, not me."

So Earwig stirred the mixture and listened carefully to all the strange words and noises Thomas made. She tried to say each one exactly the same way, which was not easy. Some of the sounds were very odd. But she thought the spell was working. The mixture had been sort of pink when she tipped all the different parts into the bowl, but as she stirred and spoke it turned colourless and smelled faintly of roses. She was very surprised that when Thomas stopped speaking, he toppled suddenly over on his back and writhed about on the table with all his paws waving. "What's wrong?" she asked anxiously.

"Nothing!" Thomas said, in a kind of curdled purr. "It's just – it's just – some of the sounds were me swearing because I couldn't remember the words!"

Earwig realised he was laughing, in the way cats laugh. "Well I just hope it works," she said. "What do I do now? Spread it all over me?"

Chapter Four

Thomas sprang on to all four paws
again rather quickly. "Yes, but you do
me first," he said. "I've worked as hard
as you did. And I've had enough of her
giving me worms when she's annoyed."

This seemed fair enough. Earwig
took two big fingerfuls of the colourless
paste and rubbed them carefully into
Thomas until his black coat was
plastered wetly to his skin all over.
Thomas crouched in a hump, with his fur
sticking up in spikes. "Yeurgh!" he said,
shaking a front paw disgustedly. "I hope
it soaks in or something."

It seemed to soak in. By the time
Earwig was nearly through rubbing the
mixture all over herself – very sparingly,
because the paste got less and less
horribly quickly – Thomas shook himself

and was once more his sleek, plushy self.
"That's better!" he said. He stuck up a
back leg and washed, while Earwig
wiped her dirty feet with a rag and
spread the last of the paste over her soles
and between her toes.

"Do you think it will work?" she said.

"Flmph," said Thomas. His mouth
was full of fur. "It had better work. I'm
not going through all that again!"

"Neither am I!" said Earwig, when at
last she yawned her way back to bed. It
took ages to clear up and put all the
things back so that Bella Yaga would not

guess any of them had been used. After
that she had to wash the slime off her
feet and then clean the slimy footprints
off the hall floor. Earwig nearly fell
asleep on the floor while she was doing
that.

And, naturally, it only seemed five
minutes after she had fallen asleep that
Bella Yaga was banging on her door and
shouting.

"Get up, you lazy little beast! The
Mandrake wants his bacon and eggs."

"Tell him to get a demon to do it,"
Earwig growled.

"*What?*" screamed Bella Yaga.

"I'm *coming!*" Earwig shouted back. "And I'm not your slave!"

"That's what you think!" Bella Yaga yelled.

Chapter Five

Not surprisingly, Earwig was in a very
bad temper that day. She grumbled
under her breath while she worked in the
workroom, and she grumbled out loud
when she had to trudge out to the

Chapter Five

weed-garden to fetch nettles and
hellebore. "I've had enough of being
treated like a slave!" she said. "And it's
raining!" She trudged back and threw
the wet plants down on the table.

"Don't do that!" snapped Bella Yaga.
"I told you to put the plants in the
cauldron, you useless little beast!"

"And I told you I'm not your slave!"
Earwig snapped back. "I agreed to be
your assistant and you agreed to teach
me magic, and all you've done is work
me half to death!"

"I did not agree to teach you magic!"

Bella Yaga shouted. "I got you from St Morwald's because I needed another pair of hands!"

"Then you're a cheat!" Earwig said. "You cheated Mrs Briggs and you cheated me. You told Mrs Briggs you were going to be my Foster Mother."

Bella Yaga glared at Earwig. She was in such a rage that her brown eye turned upwards and her blue eye turned down. Earwig was quite frightened and wondered if she had gone too far. But all Bella Yaga did was to slap Earwig round the head so hard that her ears rang. "Foster Mother indeed!" she said, laughing angrily. "Go and put more fuel under the cauldron. Now. Or I'll give you worms."

Earwig went giddily over to the

mound of sludge where the green flames
were and piled sticks under the cauldron.
When her head had cleared a little, she
said, "Well? Are you going to teach me
magic or not?"

"Of course not," said Bella Yaga.
"You're only my spare pair of hands."

Right! Earwig thought. *That does it!*

Earwig seethed with rage for the rest
of the morning, but she took care to
seethe quietly so that Bella Yaga would
not see how angry she was. Lunch was
the specially nice shepherd's pie that the
cook at St Morwald's used to make

Earwig as a special treat. The
Mandrake had made his demons fetch it
because he liked it too. Earwig could
scarcely believe it when she recognised
it. She stared at her plate and could
hardly eat for anger and homesickness.

After lunch, Bella Yaga gathered up
all the spells from the last few days, put
each one carefully in a plastic bag and
packed all the bags in a shopping
basket. She unhooked her red hat from
the hall and put it on her head. "I'm off
to deliver these to my customers," she
said.

In spite of being so angry, Earwig was interested enough to ask, "Do you go on a broomstick?"

"Certainly not," said Bella Yaga. "All my customers are very respectable. They belong to Friends of the Earth and the Mothers' Union. They'd have fits if their neighbours saw me arrive on a broomstick! Now stop asking stupid questions and get the floor in here clean. I want to be able to eat my dinner off it when I come back."

Earwig watched Bella Yaga open the blank wall at the end of the hall just as if

it was a front door and go out. As soon
as the wall slammed shut, Earwig raced
back to the workroom, calling for
Thomas.

"What is it?" Thomas asked
grumpily, struggling out from one of the
mixing bowls. "I was asleep. The only
time I get any peace is when she goes
out."

"Yes, I know," Earwig said. "But just
help me for five minutes. What's a spell
for giving someone another pair of
hands?"

Thomas's foot stopped halfway to

irritably scratching his chin. "*What* a good idea!" he said respectfully. "Let's look in her book."

The only spell in the book that was anything like what Earwig had in mind was called *To Make Extra Growth on a Person's Body.* "Do you think it might do?" she asked Thomas.

"Just about," Thomas said, crouched over the page. "The real difficulty is how to get a hair of her head to put in the image. She won't let you near her hair if she can help it."

"I'll get one somehow," Earwig said

grimly. "She keeps saying she wants another pair of hands. She's going to get them if it kills me!"

Earwig worked feverishly for the next hour. The spell told her to make an image of the person out of all sorts of unpleasant things. Then you made the extra bits you wanted out of bats' wings and beeswax and stuck that on with Thomas standing by as familiar. The thing that made the spell work was a hair from the head of the person you were working on, wrapped round the image.

Earwig enjoyed making a model of
Bella Yaga. She ran to the bathroom
from time to time to look at her picture,
to make sure she was getting it ugly
enough. But she had trouble with the

spare pair of hands. They were so tiny. She had to roll them up and start again three times. Then when at last she got them right, she could not decide on the best place to put them.

"Do you think on her elbows?" she asked Thomas.

"On her knees?" Thomas suggested. "She—" He stopped and stood up in an arch with all his fur on end. "Hide it! Quick! She's coming back!"

Earwig could not hear anything, but she knew animals' ears were far better than humans'. She did not argue. She stuck the two tiny hands on anywhere in order not to lose them. She scooped up the image – and a big screwdriver with it, because of another idea she had had – and ran with it all to her bedroom. She pushed the model and the screwdriver under her pillow and ran back to the workroom. There was just time to get a broom and start pushing it about before Bella Yaga came in.

"Do you call that floor clean?" Bella Yaga said. "You don't get any supper unless you do better than that, you lazy creature!"

Earwig had to sweep and scrape and
scrub for the rest of the day. But she was
so busy thinking of ways to get a hair
from Bella Yaga's head that she hardly
noticed what she was doing. She thought
if she could only find Bella Yaga's
bedroom, it would be easy. There would
be a comb or a hairbrush on the
dressing-table and there would be hair
in those. Bella Yaga never tidied
anything up.

By supper time the floor was almost
clean, but not quite. Bella Yaga grinned
meanly. "You can go to your bedroom

and have bread and cheese for supper there," she said. "That might teach you not to be so lazy in the future!"

Earwig ran to her room, hoping to see the demon who brought the bread and cheese. But it was a little disappointing. *Something* certainly came into the room. There was a whirling wind and a feeling of hotness. But all Earwig *saw* was a plate of Ploughman's Lunch from the pub down the road, which suddenly appeared in the middle of her bed, and the whirling stopped as soon as she saw it.

"Are you there?" said Earwig. But nothing was.

After she had eaten the Ploughman's Lunch – it was quite filling, with two kinds of pickle and a hardboiled egg as well as cheese and French bread – Earwig thoughtfully took the screwdriver from under her pillow. She knelt down by the wall that was supposed to have the bathroom on the other side and started to make a hole in it with the screwdriver. Thomas had said that the Mandrake's room was on the other side. It stood to reason that Bella

Yaga's room was there too. So Earwig
bored and twiddled and scraped with the
screwdriver, until she felt the end of it come
loose into air on the other side of the wall.
Then, very slowly and gently, scarcely
daring to breathe, she pulled the
screwdriver out and put her eye to the
hole.

A hotness blew in her eye. She had to
wipe plaster dust out of it before she
could look again. When she had,
she found she was not looking
at a bedroom. Nor was it
the bathroom. It seemed to

104

be a kind of study through there, painted
in black and gold and red. The huge
figure of the Mandrake was nearby,
sitting at some kind of desk.
Beyond him was a
whirling, writhing
Something.

Earwig could only see bits of the something, but she was fairly sure it was a demon. And if it *was* a demon, she knew she did not want to see a demon ever again. She took her eye away and plugged up the hole with the screwdriver.

"Bother!" she said. This did not get her any nearer to getting hold of one of Bella Yaga's hairs. She squatted on her heels, thinking. After a bit, still thinking, she got up and went to the bathroom and looked at the wall there. Sure enough, there was a little crumbly hole and she could just see the tip of the screwdriver sticking through it.

"I don't understand magic," Earwig said. "She's going to *have* to teach me about it."

Chapter Six

Next morning, Bella Yaga was screaming as usual, "Wake up! Hurry up! The Mandrake wants fried bread for breakfast today!"

Earwig shot out of bed, shot into her

clothes and shot to the hall to go to the bathroom. There she came to a dead stop and stood staring at Bella Yaga's red hat, hanging on its peg.

"Of course!" she said. "I bet there's a hair in that hat!"

Quickly, she unhooked the hat and, sure enough, there were two hairs, curly and blue-purple, clinging to the hatband inside.

Earwig picked them off and raced to the bathroom, where she hid them in her sponge bag.

"Hurry up!" screamed Bella Yaga.

You wait! Earwig thought. She hurried to the kitchen and put some slices of bread in the frying pan. The bread drank all the fat in the pan and then it burnt, in spite of Earwig pouring in what felt like a gallon more fat as it cooked.

The Mandrake stared at the plate of dry, black slices. "What is this?" He turned his eyes to Earwig. She saw the red sparks lighting up in them.

"I've never done fried bread before," she said. "Isn't it right?"

"No," said the Mandrake. The burning pits of his eyes turned to Bella Yaga. "Why didn't you teach her how?"

Bella Yaga went pale. "Well, I – er – anyone can cook fried bread."

"Wrong," said the Mandrake. "Don't let it disturb me again." He waved his hand. There was a sort of wavering in the air over his left shoulder. A sweet voice spoke out of nowhere.

"How can I serve my hideous master today?"

"Don't be rude," growled the Mandrake. "You can take this food away and get me some real fried bread from the Scout Camp in Epping Forest."

"Yes, ghastly master," the voice said. The wobbling air whirled. In the time it took Earwig to blink, the burnt bread had gone and there were golden crisp slices on the plate instead. The Mandrake grunted and began to eat then in terrible, powerful silence. Bella Yaga kept very quiet too. Earwig saw that Thomas had crawled away to hide behind the wastebucket under the sink,

so she wisely said nothing either.
Breakfast seemed to go on for a year.

When it was over at last, Bella Yaga
hurried Earwig to the workroom. "How
dare you disturb the Mandrake like
that!" she scolded. "You nearly had me
in bad trouble!"

"Well, you should try to teach me
things instead of just
making me do them,"
Earwig said.

"Don't give me silly
excuses!" said Bella
Yaga. "You're here to

work. I told you I need another pair of hands."

You'll get them! Earwig thought fiercely.

They started work. When enough time had passed to make it seem likely, Earwig said, "I need to go to the toilet."

"Anything to annoy me!" said Bella Yaga. "All right. You can have exactly two minutes. Any longer and I give you worms."

Earwig raced away to the bathroom and collected the two hairs from her sponge bag. She raced to her bedroom. In a terrible hurry, she lifted up the pillow, planted the two hairs on the little image of Bella Yaga and raced back to the bathroom to pull the chain. She sped back to the workroom.

There was a terrible howl as she opened the door. Thomas shot between Earwig's legs and dived into her bedroom out of sight.

"What have you done?" Bella Yaga was shrieking. "You wicked girl, what have you *done*?"

Earwig put both hands over her

mouth in order not to laugh out loud. She had not noticed where she had stuck the extra hands on. She had been in too much of a hurry. One had ended up stuck to Bella Yaga's forehead. It flapped there, with its fingers opening and shutting in front of Bella Yaga's eyes. As Earwig looked, its finger and thumb found Bella Yaga's nose and pinched. Bella Yaga howled and spun round. The other hand, to Earwig's great pleasure, was stuck to the back of Bella Yaga's tweed skirt like a tail. That was pinching her too.

"Whad hab you dud?" Bella Yaga yelled again, trying to wrench the finger and thumb away from her nose.

"Given you an extra pair of hands," Earwig said. "Just like you said you wanted."

"Ooh!" howled Bella Yaga. "I'll gib you wurbs!"

Earwig found herself being pushed and hurried backwards. It was like being swept by an invisible broom. The pushing landed her inside her bedroom and shut the door on her with a slam. Earwig heard the lock click and knew she was locked in this time. She turned round and saw Thomas standing on her bed, looped into a hoop, with his fur on end and his eyes staring.

"Stay there!" Bella Yaga screamed from outside. "Stay there with wurbs!"

Thomas gave a long and trembling howl and dived under the covers of

Earwig's bed. There he crawled and pushed and scrambled until he was a small, very flat hump right down at the very end.

"You don't need to hide," Earwig said to him. "We did that spell. She can't hurt us."

But Thomas clearly had no faith in the spell at all. He stayed where he was and would not speak or move, even when Earwig prodded him. She sighed and sat on her bed to see what would happen about the worms.

After a minute or so, the image of

Bella Yaga flew out from under the pillow and flopped on the floor. Earwig saw that the two little hands had come loose. She picked up the image and tried to stick the hands back on. She tried them in several places, but nothing seemed to make them stick. Earwig sighed again, because she knew that Bella Yaga had somehow broken the spell completely.

Then the worms arrived. They appeared in a big, wriggling bundle out of nowhere and fell to the floor by Earwig's feet. Earwig pulled her feet out of their way and stared down at them. There seemed to be at least a hundred of them. They were the size of earthworms and, as Bella Yaga had promised, they were blue and purple and very wriggly. The wriggliness, Earwig saw, was because the worms were not happy out on the bare floor. Some of them were trying to wriggle down the cracks in the floorboards to get out of the daylight.

"Our spell works," Earwig told the hump that was Thomas. "The worms are on the floor, not doing any harm at all."

The hump refused to move or speak.

"Scaredy cat!" said Earwig. "You're

worse than Custard."

But since Thomas still refused to speak or come out, Earwig sat and thought about the worms. They did not worry her at all, for being worms. But something worried her. After a while, she knew what it was. Those worms were supposed to be inside her. If Bella Yaga found out they were on the floor instead, she would know that Earwig and Thomas had worked the spell to keep themselves safe. And then Bella Yaga would break that spell at once.

Earwig wondered how to hide the worms. The only hiding place in the room was inside the bed and, since Thomas was so scared of worms, that was not kind. But – Earwig's eyes went to the screwdriver still sticking out of the wall. That hole she had made was exactly the right size to take a worm. Bella Yaga never seemed to go near the bathroom, so the worms could creep under the bathmat and stay hidden there until Bella Yaga decided to let Earwig out. Then she could put them in a bucket and take them out into the weed-garden, where they would be happier.

Earwig got up and pulled the

screwdriver out of the wall. Then she picked up the nearest blue wriggling worm and coaxed it into the hole. The worm went in eagerly. It really hated being out on the floor. As soon as it was through, Earwig picked up the next, and the next. She put worm after worm through the wall, feeling as if she was doing a good deed. Everyone was much happier like this, and Bella Yaga need never know.

She was feeding the last worm through the hole when Thomas crawled out from under the bedclothes. "What are you doing?" he said.

"Sending the worms to hide in the bathroom," Earwig explained.

"No!" yowled Thomas and went back under the bedclothes like a rat up a drainpipe.

"Honestly, Custard – I mean, Thomas!" Earwig said, as she let go of the last worm's tail. "Anyone would think—"

The wall turned red hot.

Earwig got to the other side of the room quicker even than Thomas had got down inside the bed. There was a growling from behind the red-hot wall that very quickly rose to a howling and then a roaring. Earwig covered her ears. As she did, most of the wall vanished and the Mandrake stormed through. He was alight with black fire and taller than

ever. His eyes were red pits of rage. Dark
fire streamed backwards from the horns
on his head.

Earwig found herself crouched under
her bed without knowing how she got
there.

"Worms!" bellowed the Mandrake.
"I'LL GIVE HER WORMS!"

From under the bed Earwig saw his
huge feet, which now seemed to have
claws on them, make smoking holes in
the floor as he marched across her
bedroom and out through the wall
beside the door. A roaring and rushing

filled the air behind him. Peeping from where she crouched, Earwig saw scaly paws, ratty tails, slimy hooves, horny wingtips and many queerer things that were parts of the host of demons following the Mandrake. She did not try to see all of any of them. In fact some of them made her hide her face in her hands.

There was a huge crash as the Mandrake walked through the workroom wall. There was a noise like a thunderstorm. Earwig heard Bella Yaga shrieking, "It wasn't me! It wasn't me!"

Then she heard Bella Yaga shrieking
angry spells. Then there was a crashing,
and Bella Yaga was just shrieking.
Earwig saw flickers of green and black
light.

Then there was quiet. It was not a
good quiet. Earwig stayed where she
was. She did not move, nor take her
hands from her face, even when she
heard her bedroom door open.

"Come out," said the Mandrake.

Earwig crawled out, very slowly. To
her surprise, there were no burnt patches
in the floor and no kind of holes in the

 132

walls. The Mandrake was standing in the doorway looking like an ordinary man in a bad mood, except for the little red sparks in the middle of his eyes.

"She gave you worms," he said.

"Yes," said Earwig, "and I put them into the bathroom to hide. It was a mistake."

"Magic worms go through into a magic place," the Mandrake said. "They went into my den. She won't do that to you again. You won't do that again. I've told her she's to make you a proper assistant and teach you properly. I don't like being disturbed."

"Thank you," said Earwig. "Could you make her send me to school tomorrow too, when term starts? I need to see my friend Custard."

"Maybe," said the Mandrake. He walked across to the wall where Earwig had made the hole.

"The bungalow will be much more peaceful if I'm out all day," Earwig pointed out quickly.

"I'll think about it," said the Mandrake. He walked into the wall and vanished.

"Oh well," said Earwig. She turned

round and dug Thomas out from under

the bedclothes. He lay heavy and soft in
her arms. Earwig put her face on his fur
and he began to purr. Earwig smiled.
She thought about what had just
happened. "You know," she told Thomas,
"if I work things out right, we ought to
be able to make both of them behave just
the way we want them to."

She carried Thomas across the hall to
the workroom. Bella Yaga, looking red
and harried, was picking up broken glass
and bits of mixing bowls. She turned her
blue eye nastily in Earwig's direction.
Earwig said quickly, before Bella Yaga

could speak, "Please, I've come for my
first magic lesson."

Bella Yaga sighed angrily. "All right,"
she said. "You win – for now. But I wish I
knew how you did it!"

*****

A year went by.

*****

Earwig sighed happily as she woke up
and tried to get her toes from under fat
Thomas. Everyone in her new home now
did exactly what she told them to do. It
was almost better than the orphanage.
The Mandrake had even taken to calling
her Dearwig. When Earwig asked him

to tell his demons to fetch her breakfast,
the demons fetched it at once. They were
beginning to do what Earwig told them
to do without her having to ask the
Mandrake first. Yesterday they had
brought her the breakfast menu from the
best hotel in town. Earwig picked it up
and studied it.

Breakfast in bed with kippers, she
thought, *or scrambled eggs, or why not
both?* While she was wondering whether
or not to have yogurt as well, she
remembered the only sad thing in her
life. Nothing would induce Custard to

come and visit her. He was much too
afraid of the Mandrake. Still, she
thought, deciding to have the mixed grill
after all, she could work on Custard just
as she had worked on her new household.

DIANA WYNNE JONES'S first children's book was published in 1973. Her magical, humorous stories have enthralled children and adults ever since, and she has inspired many of today's children's and fantasy authors. Among Diana's best-loved books for older children are the Chrestomanci series and the Howl books. Her novel *Howl's Moving Castle* was made into an award-winning film. She was described by Neil Gaiman as "the best children's writer of the last forty years".